SAM AND SPOT

COOL KIDS
PRESS

Boca Raton, Florida

A SILLY STORY

by John O'Brien

ISBN: 1-56790-500-5

First Printing

COOL KIDS PRESS

1098 N.W. Boca Raton Boulevard, Suite 1
Boca Raton, FL 33432

Printed in Singapore

O'Brien, John, 1953-
 Sam and Spot : a silly story / John O'Brien.
   p. cm.
 Summary: Sam has trouble locating his dog Spot in this story made up of words beginning with the letter S.
  ISBN 1-56790-500-5
  [1. Dogs--Fiction.] I. Title.
PZ7.O12687Sam 1994
[E]--dc20   94-26643
                CIP
                AC

For Tess

One sunny Saturday, Sam and Spot strolled in the square.

Sam and Spot stopped -- Sam to sit and snooze, and Spot to sniff and snoop.

Spot scatted.

Sam stirred and saw Spot had strayed.

Sam stood and shouted, "Spot!"

In seconds, Sam was surrounded by a slew of Spots of all sizes and shapes.

Sam searched the slew of Spots for his special Spot, but was stumped.

So Sam said, "My Spot sports a single spot."

A Spot with several spots skedaddled.

Then Sam said, "My Spot sports shoes and socks."

Soon a shoe-and-sockless Spot split.

Again Sam spoke. "My Spot sports sun shades."

A sad Spot without sun shades separated.

"My Spot is sleek and slim," Sam stressed.

A stocky Spot stole away.

"My Spot sports a scarf," said Sam.

A scarfless Spot slipped out silently.

Sam said, "My Spot sports a sombrero."

Sporting no sombrero, a Spot split.

Still striving to select his Spot, Sam spoke. "My Spot is shorter in stature."

A seventh Spot sadly slunk away.

Since a single Spot still stood, Sam was sure he saw his special Spot.

Sam smiled. But Spot seemed sorry for the six or seven Spots
sadly seeking their own special Sams.

So Spot shouted, "Sam!"

A slew of Sams of all shapes and sizes strode to the scene.

Special Spots selected special Sams and special Sams selected special Spots.
All the Sams and Spots smiled and sang and all was sunny.